Belle Is My Babysitter

By Victoria Saxon and Andrea Posner-Sanchez

Illustrated by Fabio Laguna and Meritxell Andreu

🌱 A GOLDEN BOOK • NEW YORK

randomhousekids.com
ISBN 978-0-7364-3502-4 (trade) — ISBN 978-0-7364-3503-1 (ebook)
Printed in the United States of America
10 9 8 7 6 5 4

One day, Mrs. Potts visited Belle in the castle library.

"I'm going to be busy in the kitchen all day," Mrs. Potts said. "Would you mind babysitting Chip?"

"I'd be delighted," replied Belle.

Mrs. Potts hopped over to whisper in Belle's ear. "Thank you, dear. I'm afraid he's a bit grumpy today."

Chip frowned. "Today is field day for all the village kids," he said. "I can't play because I'm a teacup."

"I'm sorry you're sad," Belle said, "but I'm sure there are still lots of fun things you can do."

Chip thought for a moment. "Well, I can blow bubbles," he said. "Wanna see?" He hopped out of the library and stopped near Cogsworth, who was supervising the castle staff as they cleaned the hallway.

"Fill me up, please," Chip said.

Chip took a deep breath. He closed his eyes and blew. Mounds of bubbles started to flow over his face.

"Well done!" shouted Belle.

"Don't get the fresh wax wet!" cried Cogsworth.

"Head outside with such silliness!"

Belle giggled as she carried Chip to the patio. "I can blow bubbles, too," she told him. She tied the ends of a piece of string together. Then she dunked it in a bucket of soapy water.

She stretched the string out and slowly blew an enormous bubble.

"Wow!" Excited, Chip hopped into the air—
and popped the bubble.

"Now there are two fun things you can do,"
Belle said. "You can blow bubbles and pop them."

"Yeah, but bubbles aren't a field day event,"
he complained.

That gave Belle an idea. She'd make a field day for Chip and the other enchanted objects right there in the castle.

FIELD DAY TODAY AT 2:00

The first event was sugar-cube catching. Belle thought
Chip and his siblings would do well—teacups were used to
having sugar cubes dropped into them!

"Let's have the spoons line up on one side of the table,"
Belle said. "Everyone else should go on the other side,
facing the spoons."

At the count of three, the spoons began to launch sugar cubes. Cogsworth got bopped in the face a few times. The cups were more successful. They quickly hopped around, making some good catches. Before long, Chip was filled to the rim with sugar!

"Chip is the winner!" Belle announced.

Next, everyone went to the library. Belle had set up an obstacle course of books.

"Who wants to go first?" Belle asked.

Featherduster had a good start but got caught under a low bridge.

Lumiere tripped over a book and almost started a fire!

Luckily, Chip raced over to extinguish the flames.

"Well, I guess we don't have a winner for the obstacle course," Belle said.

"Ah, but we do have a winner—for bravest boy!" Lumiere declared, beaming at Chip.

The next event was riding Footstool, who was as jumpy as a bucking bronco. It would be tough to stay on and cross the finish line! Cogsworth fell off after just a few seconds.

FINISH

The spoons fell off.

Featherduster fell off.

Chip fell off, too! But they all had a lot of fun.

Footstool was still full of energy.

"You try, Belle!" Chip insisted.

Belle sat down and enjoyed a wild ride.

Mrs. Potts came outside to tell everyone to get ready to serve dinner. She was happy to see that Chip was no longer a grumpy teacup.

"You're a wonderful friend," she told Belle.

"And this was the best field day ever!" Chip cheered.